The Time of the Pharaohs

Half and Half

GREAT STORY & COOL FACTS

Introduction

Welcome to Half and Half books, a great combination of story and facts! You might want to read this book on your own. However, the section with real facts is a little more difficult to read than the story. You might find it helpful to read the facts section with your parent, or someone else, who can help you with the more difficult words. Your parent may also be able to answer any questions you have about the facts—or at least help you find more information!

The Time of the Pharaohs

Special thanks to Dr. Cathleen Keller, Associate Professor of Egyptology, University of California, Berkeley, for her review and invaluable suggestions for this book.

English Edition Copyright © 2008 by Treasure Bay, Inc.
English Edition translated by Elizabeth Bell and edited by Sindy McKay

Original Edition Copyright © 2002 by Nathan / VUEF, Paris–France
Original Edition: Au temps des pharaons

Meri's Daring Adventure by Alain Surget,
Illustrated by Philippe de Kemmeter

Non-fiction text by Corinne Le Dour Zana
Non-fiction illustrations by Pascal Baltzer, Buster Bone and Francesca D'Ottavi

Photography Credits
Cover: Bridgeman Giraudon; p. 30–31: G. Dagli Orti/Archives Larbor;
p. 34: G. Dagli Orti; p. 38: h: T. Perrin/Hoa-Qui; bg: Scala; bd: Scala;
p. 39 hg; G. Dagli Orti; hd: P. Sonneville/Archives Nathan; b: G. Dagli Orti;
p. 42–43: M. Guittet/Nathan

Published by Treasure Bay, Inc.
40 Sir Francis Drake Boulevard
San Anselmo, CA 94960 USA

PRINTED IN SINGAPORE

Library of Congress Catalog Card Number: 2007937979

Hardcover ISBN-13: 978-1-60115-201-5
Paperback ISBN-13: 978-1-60115-202-2

Visit us online at:
www.HalfAndHalfBooks.com

J-nf

The Time of the Pharaohs

Table of Contents

Facts: Ancient Eygpt

Meri's Daring Adventure

Story by **Alain Surget**
Illustrated by **Philippe de Kemmeter**

1

The Stone Hill

Meri sat with her father, Nefer, gazing at the flooded fields before them. The evening sun sparkled on the water with a fiery glow. Two weeks ago, the river Nile had spilled over its banks and flooded their fields. The mighty river had done this every year since before they could remember.

As they gazed across the water, they saw the huge stone structure at the edge of the desert. Eight years ago, when Meri had been born, it had already reached high into the sky.

"The pyramid is almost finished," Nefer told his daughter. "Tomorrow I must cross the river to help complete it."

"I would love to see the pyramid up close!" Meri exclaimed. "May I come with you?"

Nefer shook his head. "The work site is no place for children."

"Please? I wouldn't be any trouble."

"No, Meri," Nefer said firmly. "It's too dangerous."

Meri wrinkled her brow in worry. "Is it too dangerous for you too, Father?"

Nefer chuckled as he answered, "Not as long as I'm wearing my lucky headband!"

2

The Dangers of the Nile

The next morning, Meri awoke to find her father already gone. She wished she could have gone with him. Then she spotted something on the breakfast table. Her father's lucky headband!

"He won't be safe without it," she thought. "I must take it to him!"

Meri ran down to the banks of the Nile and climbed into an old fishing boat. She began making her way across the Nile. Suddenly, the water started churning around her. Her boat rocked and shook. A huge gray back rose from the depths like a giant rock. A hippopotamus!

Meri watched in fear as another surfaced! And another!

Meri began to row with all her might. She knew that she and her tiny boat were no match for the incredible power of an angry hippopotamus!

As she rowed past one of the hippos, it opened its enormous mouth. Its teeth looked as long as swords. Meri rowed even faster. She heard the mouth snap shut just behind her. Then the animal dove beneath the water and disappeared. Shaken but safe, Meri continued toward the opposite shore.

Up ahead, she noticed a greenish tree trunk floating toward her through the reeds.

She used an oar to push the tree trunk out of her way. That's when she spied an eye on the trunk, staring up at her. It wasn't a tree trunk after all. It was a crocodile!

Meri froze, not moving a muscle. The crocodile swam around her boat in circles, moving closer and closer. Terrified, Meri closed her eyes and waited for the croc to overturn her with one slap of its mighty tail. She waited and waited.

Finally, she opened her eyes and looked around. The crocodile was gone! She sighed in relief and began rowing again. Nothing could make her turn back now.

3

At the Foot of the Pyramid

At last, Meri reached the shore near the pyramid. She had never seen such confusion. Workers were everywhere, shouting to one another. The braying of donkeys mixed with the sound of hammers and axes on stone. The air was filled with a thick yellow dust. It stung her eyes and made her cough. She saw an endless line of yellow blocks being pulled by weary workers.

Meri began working her way through the crowd, searching for her father. Workmen shoved her out of the way. Donkeys almost stepped on her. Splinters of stone flew past, almost hitting her.

At last, Meri arrived at the pyramid and stared up at it in awe. It looked like a magnificent stairway to the sky.

"Move!" shouted a worker.

"You shouldn't be here!" shouted another.

Meri tried to stay clear of the workers, but couldn't. Everywhere she turned, someone was yelling at her. She wished there was someplace she could hide.

Suddenly, she spotted a big white tent off to the side.

Meri ran to the back of the tent, lifted the edge, and slipped inside.

Inside was a young man. He was lying on some pillows, fast asleep. His helmet rested atop a tall spear. Leopard skins covered the ground.

Meri suddenly realized how tired she was from her adventure. She moved to lie down on one of the skins—but stopped when she saw something stir beneath it. She jerked the skin aside to see what it was.

Sssss! A black cobra reared up and spread its hood, ready to strike. Meri jumped back in terror. Bang! She knocked into the spear. Klonk! The helmet fell off and landed on the snake's head, killing it instantly.

The young man on the pillows awoke with a start. "Who's there?" he thundered.

The young man wore a golden necklace. On it was an image of the sun. Meri knew that there was only one person in all of Egypt who had the right to wear such a necklace.

"Pha—Pharaoh?" she stammered.

Pharaoh strode toward her, his face stiff with anger. "What are you doing in my tent?" He was about to grab her and throw her out when he saw the lifeless snake on the ground. The look on his face changed instantly. "Did you kill this snake?" he asked.

"I'm sorry," answered Meri. "I was just looking for my father and—"

"You saved my life," exclaimed the Pharaoh. "Just tell me what you wish and you will have it!"

4

The Stone Portrait

The Pharaoh's guards ordered all the workers to line up outside the tent. The stone cutters were in one row. The donkey drivers were in another. The men who hauled the blocks of stone were in the last.

They all watched in silent awe as Meri and Pharaoh walked out of the tent together. "Who is the father of this child?" Pharaoh asked in a booming voice.

After a moment, Nefer stepped forward. "Meri is my daughter," he answered nervously.

Pharaoh signaled for Nefer to come closer.

Nefer knelt before his king.

"Stand up," Pharaoh ordered. "Today your daughter saved my life. In honor of this deed, her face will be carved on the wall inside my pyramid. In this way, she will protect me through the centuries, as she has protected me today."

Nefer smiled proudly as the crowd cheered.

Pharaoh turned to Meri. "How else can I repay you?" he asked.

Meri shyly responded, "May I visit your pyramid?"

Pharaoh nodded. "Your father will be your guide."

As Nefer led his daughter toward the towering pyramid, the crowd again cheered for the little girl. "Long live Meri, protector of the Pharaoh!"

"I only came here to bring you your lucky headband, Father," Meri whispered to her father with a smile. "And now my face is to be carved into the pyramid wall!"

"I told you that headband was lucky," Nefer whispered back to her.

He took her hand and Meri's smile grew even wider as they entered the Pharaoh's tomb . . .

The Nile River

Many historians believe that the first humans arrived in Egypt after crossing the Sahara Desert in search of water. These early people settled on the banks of the Nile where they founded a great kingdom.

The country's wealth comes from the Nile. The Nile River allowed early Egyptians to grow grains, fruit, and beans. They were also able to fish from its banks—despite the hippos and crocodiles! Muddy clay from the river was used to make pottery and bricks for building. Plants growing on its shore were used to make paper, sandals, and baskets.

Each year, heavy rains caused the Nile to overflow its banks. This kept the soil around the river very healthy. To protect villages, many dikes and dams were built.

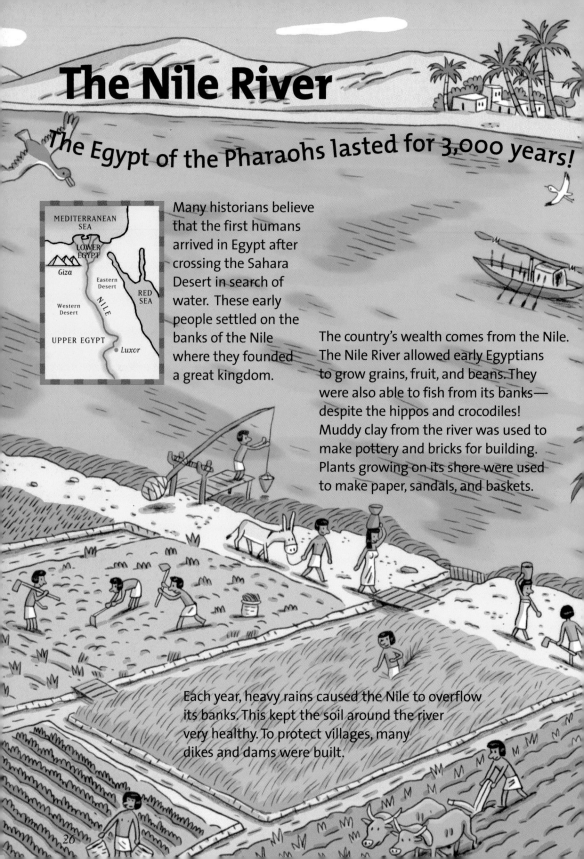

26

Egypt was ruled by the pharaoh. He was the king of Egypt and was worshipped as a god. Beneath the pharaoh were the priests, the scribes, and the military generals. Next came the doctors, engineers, and soldiers. Many more people were merchants, servants, and craftspeople. Most people, however, were laborers and farmers.

The pharaoh held all the power. He ruled the country with the help of his close advisor called a tjaty. The pharaoh lived in a great palace with his family and many servants. On important occasions, the pharaoh would wear special clothing. This included a fake beard and the pschent (skent), which is a double crown representing the union of Upper and Lower Egypt.

The Egypt of the pharaohs

| 3000 BC | *Cheops* (kē´ops)
Ancient Empire
2700-2200 BC | *Mentuhotep*
Middle Empire
2000-1650 BC | *Amenhotep*
New Empire
1550-1070 BC | 332 BC |

Ra, king of the gods. He was often shown in the form of the sun, which was thought to die and be reborn every day.

Hathor, the goddess of love. She was sometimes shown in the form of a cow.

Thoth (thōth), the god of writing and the sciences. He is often seen with the head of a baboon or an *ibis*.

Anubis, (ə noo´ bis), the god of *embalming*. With the head of a jackal, he watched over the dead.

Gods in Heaven and

Ancient Egyptians believed that gods watche

The Egyptians worshipped more than 500 gods! Paintings and sculptures often show the gods with human bodies and animal heads. Sometimes, the gods simply appear as animals. The animals connected to the gods were considered sacred.

Each god was both kind and cruel. For example, the lioness **Sekhmet** (sek´ met) was considered a goddess of disease and plague. But when she was honored and appeased, she could also heal.

Bastet, daughter of Rê. This cat goddess protected human beings.

Horus, god of the sky, son of Isis (ī´sis) and Osiris (ō sī´ris). He had the head of a falcon and his eyes were the moon and the sun.

Osiris, god of the dead. He is shown wearing a headpiece of reeds and ostrich plumes.

Isis, wife of Osiris. She represented The protective mother.

arth

ver their world

Certain gods were thought to step in at important moments in life. **Tawaret,** the hippopotamus goddess, helped women during childbirth. The Egyptians may have seen how fiercely a hippopotamus protects her own babies.

The Death and Rebirth of Osiris

Osiris was named king of the gods by his grandfather Ra. This made his brother Seth very jealous. Seth set a trap for Osiris, shut him up in a wooden box, and threw him into the Nile. Upon his death, Osiris became the ruler and judge of the kingdom of the dead. His statues often show him wrapped in cloth like a mummy, wearing the crown of Upper Egypt and holding a whip and crook.

A House for the Gods

The Egyptians believed that every event that happened in the world was controlled by the gods. They believed the pharaoh king was the closest thing to a human god and could speak directly to every other god. The only other humans who could speak directly to the gods were the priests.

The gods were honored three times a day, but the morning ritual was the most important. The priest would enter the temple where a statue of the god was kept and use incense (a kind of perfume that is burned) to purify the air. He would then clean and dress the statue. Finally, he would offer specially prepared food and drink to the statue.

The Egyptians pa

It was very important to keep the temple pure. So the priests shaved their heads and bodies and washed often. They dressed in linen. This was the only fabric allowed in the temple. When the prayers were done, they would back out, sweeping away any trace of their footsteps.

The temple at Luxor

In the temple, only the priest could go past the open courtyard, but people could ask questions of the god through the priest. The priest would then interpret signs sent by the gods. Is it wise to buy a cow? Will my child get well? A step forward meant yes. A step backward meant no.

ᴐmage to the gods in temples

On certain occasions, the statue of a god was brought out of the temple. This allowed the people to honor the god in a grand celebration. The statue was paraded through the city, carried by the priests. Musicians and dancers performed and the people cheered.

The Pyramids

Tombs that rise to the heavens.

Some pharaohs had themselves buried in gigantic pyramids. These were designed to show their power and to preserve their memory. Each year, the Nile overflowed and the farmers could not work the land. This is when the pharaoh put them to work, building his tomb.

The pyramid of the pharaoh, Cheops, towers over the Giza (gē´zə) plateau, near the city of Cairo (kī´rō). The 450 foot structure was built over 4,600 years ago. It is made up of about 2.5 million blocks of limestone. It took 20 years of hard work and great skill to build this giant tomb.

Stone blocks were made in quarries. Some pyramids were built near a quarry. For other pyramids, the stones had to be brought to the site by boat. Each stone weighed several tons and the workers had to raise the stones into place. The wheel had not been invented yet, so the workers had to slide the stone along ramps coated with mud. The ramps went all around the pyramid.

Inside many pyramids was a maze of hallways that led to the chambers where the pharaoh and his wife were laid to rest. Their sarcophagi (stone coffins) were filled with gold and jewels that attracted grave robbers. That is why later pharaohs were buried in secret places—like the Valley of the Kings.

Hieroglyphs include three types of signs:

① **Ideograms** (id´ē ə grams)—drawings that represent an object or express a more complex idea.

mouth   bird   basket

② **Phonograms** (fō´ nə grams)—which indicate sounds.

[r]   [ba]   [k]

The drawing of a mouth can mean the word "mouth" or the sound [r]. A small mark under the drawing means it is an ideogram, and therefore means the word "mouth".

③ **Determinatives** (di tûr´mə nə tivs)—When placed at the end of a word, these signs make the meaning more specific. For example, the word "servant" is pronounced [bak] and is written: [ba] [k]. The determinative at the end means that the servant is a man and not a woman.

[ba]   [k]

A French Egyptologist, Champollion (sham pō lē ən´), was the one to finally discover the secret of Egyptian writing, in 1822.

The Mystery

It's not easy to write with drawings!

Hieroglyphs can be read from top to bottom, bottom to top, right to left, or left to right! It all depends on what direction the people in the drawing are facing. If you see a person's right profile, you read from left to right. Egyptian hieroglyphs use around 700 different symbols. Our alphabet only uses 26 symbols!

# of Hieroglyphs

The writing masters were called scribes. To become a scribe, a young boy began studying when he was nine years old. It took five years to master the skill. It was a job that many wanted because scribes did not have to pay taxes—or work on building pyramids.

Ordinary letters were carved into stone or wood tablets. Sacred texts were painted on walls or on papyrus. Papyrus was a kind of paper made from the papyrus plant. The fibers were flattened and laid crosswise in layers to be dried in the sun. As it dried, the sap from the plant glued the fibers together to create a large sheet of paper.

The Great Journey

Preparing the dead for their eternal afterlife

When an Egyptian died, he was buried with all that his family believed he might need for his journey to the afterlife. Items such as jewels and food were placed in the tomb. A miniature boat was included to help him on his way.

It was believed that the body must be preserved for the soul to survive. This was the goal of mummification. The job of mummification was performed by an embalmer.

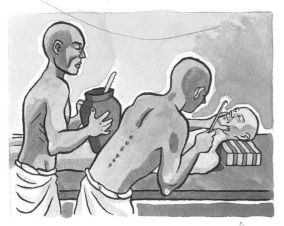

First they removed all the organs except the heart. Organs, such as the brain, contain fluid. Fluid makes the flesh rot faster.

The organs were dried and placed in jars called canopic jars. The canopic jars were then placed inside the tomb.

Next the body was dried out even more before being stuffed with cloth, so it would keep its shape. It was then coated with oils to preserve it.

The body was wrapped in bands of linen. If the cloth strips were placed end to end, the linen would be hundreds of yards long.

It took nearly 70 days to prepare a mummy. Mummification was necessary, but very expensive. It cost the average Egyptian about two months' wages.

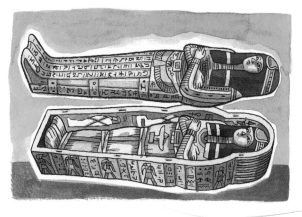

The mummy was then placed inside a sarcophagus. This stone box was decorated according to a person's rank. Once this was sealed, the deceased was ready for the journey to the kingdom of the dead, ruled by Osiris.

Upon arrival, the person would meet Osiris and be judged. Then Anubis and Thoth would weigh the person's heart on the divine scale. If good actions outweighed bad ones, the newcomer was welcomed by Osiris. If the person had behaved badly in life, his heart would be eaten by a monster.

Sphinx guarding the pyramid of Khafre (kaf´rä) at Giza

Temple of Isis on the isle of Philac

Temple of Karnak

mple of Amon at Luzor

Temple of Ramses II at Abu Simbel
(Queen Nefertari)

Remains of Ancient Eygpt

mple of Ramses II at Abu Simbel

In hieroglyphics, the owl represents the sound [M].

True or false?

True

The "pschent" is . . .

- The pharaoh's scepter
- The crown representing the union of Upper Egypt and Lower Egypt
- A type of cobra

the crown

Did You Know?

Which of these three rivers is the longest?

- The Ganges, in India
- The Nile, in Egypt
- The Amazon, in South America

The Amazon, at 4,200 miles.

Why didn't the people work their farms during the summer?

- It was too hot
- The Nile overflowed
- There were big religious celebrations to go to

The Nile overflowed.

The pyramid of Cheops was built around 2600 BC.

True or false?

True

To transport blocks of stone to build the pyramids, the Egyptians used . . .

- Carts drawn by men
- Carts drawn by horses
- Ramps coated with mud

Ramps coated with mud. When the great pyramids were built, the Egyptians did not have horses and had not discovered the wheel.

Which way do you read hieroglyphs?

- Left to right
- Right to left
- Top to bottom

Read them in the direction that the human figures are facing.

Osiris is . . .

- The king of the gods
- The god of the sciences
- The god of the dead

Osiris is the god of the dead, because he was the first to be mummified.

Pharaoh's Headddress

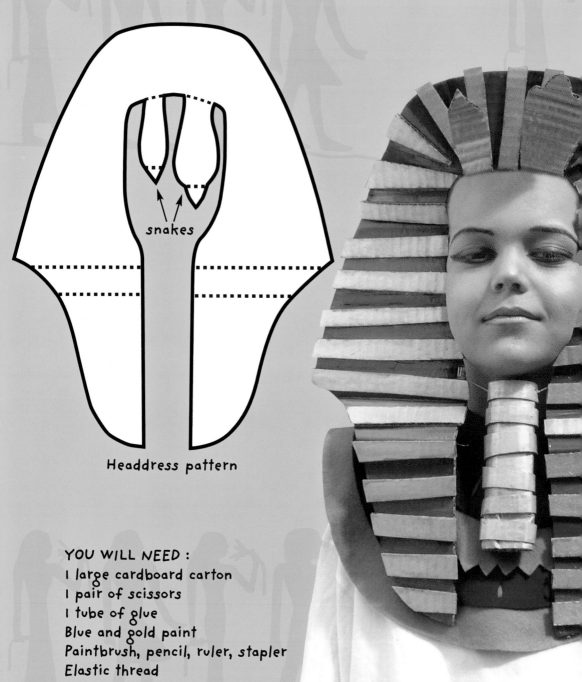

snakes

Headddress pattern

YOU WILL NEED :
1 large cardboard carton
1 pair of scissors
1 tube of glue
Blue and gold paint
Paintbrush, pencil, ruler, stapler
Elastic thread

Ask your parent to help you make Tutankhamen's headaddress for your next costume party!

1. Enlarge the headdress pattern to 400% on a photocopy machine. Trace the enlarged pattern onto the cardboard. Cut it out with scissors.

2. Cut 40 strips of cardboard, 1/2 inch by 6 1/2 inches.

3. Cut a square of cardboard about 6 by 6 inches. Roll the cardboard into a tube and hold it together with staples. (This will be the artificial beard.)

4. Crease the headdress along the dotted lines using the flat side of the ruler. Paint the entire headdress blue except for the two snakes. Paint the snakes, the tube for the beard, and the strips of cardboard gold.

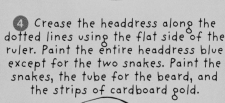

5. Glue 34 of the gold strips onto the headdress as shown in the photo. When the glue is dry, cut off the parts that stick out. Bend up the two snakes and glue them at the base so they stay up.

6. Glue the remaining 6 cardboard strips around the tube for the beard. To attach the beard, staple elastic thread to each side of the tube and to the headdress. Staple another length of elastic thread around the headdress to hold it on.

Glossary

Canopic jars (kə nop´ik) Special jars used to hold the organs of a body being mummified

Egyptologist (ē jip tol´ə jist) one who studies ancient Egypt

Embalming (em bäm´ ing) Preparing a dead body in a way that helps to preserve it

Hieroglyphics (hī rə glif´iks) The Egyptian form of writing using drawings of familiar objects

Ibis (ī´ biss) A large wading bird

Incense (in´ səns) A kind of perfume that is burned

Mummification (mum ə fə kā´ shen) The Egyptian way of preparing a dead body for burial. The job was performed by an embalmer

Papyrus (pə pī´ rəs) A kind of paper made from the papyrus plant

Pharaoh (fā´ rō) the title of ancient Egyptian kings

Pschent (skent) The double crown worn by the Pharaoh, which represented the union of Upper and Lower Egypt.

Sarcophagus (sär kofə´ gəs) Stone coffin decorated with carvings and paintings

Scribe (skrīb) writing master

If you liked **The Time of the Pharaohs**,
here is another *Half and Half™* book you are sure to enjoy!

People of the Caves

STORY: Roe's father is a great chief and he wants Roe to be a great hunter. However, Roe is more interested in understanding animals than learning how to hunt them. On an important hunt, Roe fails to spear a bison and embarrasses his father. Now, Roe has been told that he cannot eat with the tribe until he can make himself useful. Could taming a wolf be useful?

FACTS: Learn how early humans of Europe, the Cro-Magnons, lived and survived. Over 20,000 years ago, these ancient people lived a hard life that was focused primarily on hunting for food. The most advanced invention they had was a fish hook! Yet, despite their harsh life, the Cro-Magnons also created some of the first works of art: sculptures and cave paintings, many of which have survived to this day.

To see all the Half and Half books that are available,
just go online to **www.HalfAndHalf.com**